BURIED MEMORIES

KIMBERLEY SHEAD

For Roy, with love x

1

"When did you see your first dead body?"

Feigning deafness, Albie ignored the question from the female officer's colourless lips. He watched PC Darcy Nicholls, whose face, now tinged with a trace of puce-green, looked down at the grey-faced bundle on the ground. An artificial spotlight illuminated the dead body and bounced off every surface in the tight space.

It wasn't the type of question Albie was asked every day and certainly not one he was in a hurry to answer. Instead, he edged his way around the outskirts of the crime scene, head bent and shoulders rounded to compensate for the slanted low-ceilinged room. The space resembled a walk-in vertical grave dug into a cave of stones and mud. With each step, he moved further from his colleague and inched closer to the familiarity of the pathologist, Leo Nico. Leo hunched over the dead child, curled in a foetal ball, near his feet and fiddled with an evidence bag. Albie's colleague, Darcy Nicholls, stood to one side, her stare fixated on the small victim . Without looking up, Leo acknowledged Albie's presence with a nod.

"What can you tell us?" Albie asked, his full attention focused on Leo, who leaned in closer to hear the whispered question. "Is it...?"

He shook his head and waved the tweezers he held towards the victim. "The body is a young girl of a similar age to your missing child. Until I know for sure, there'll be no speculation."

Albie nodded and watched Leo as he busied himself, setting up the equipment while mumbling under his breath about the lack of space to do a proper job. Sian Wilkins had been missing for over a week, and finding her alive seemed less likely with each passing day.

A clatter from the corner drew both men's attention. Nicholls held out a hand to stop the domino effect her clumsiness had started. Her foot caught in a cable and caused a light hooked onto a nearby rock to clutter to the ground, just missing the body. This left the claustrophobic crime scene in virtual darkness.

Leo dropped his tools onto the covered floor. "Albie," he called, contorting his body he threw himself to the ground like an international goalkeeper with a point to prove, and managed to stand the light upright without interfering with the corpse or its surrounding area.

"Get her out of here before she does any actual damage!" Leo hissed and eased his body into a sitting position, methodically checking the lighting unit.

"Sorry." Darcy whispered. she reached for part of the lamp, which rolled to a stop near her feet.

"Accidents only happen once in this job, you won't make the same mistake again." Albie assured her with a pat on the back. He watched frustration flush her cheeks as she made a useless attempt to marry the thread of the metal nut. Eventually, she gave up and placed the part in Leo's out-stretched hand, then inched away as if he were a feral animal ready to attack.

Albie waited until she was within arms reach and placed his hands on her shoulders. He guided her back towards the exit of the grimy underground room and into the basement beyond.

"I don't know what—"

Albie lifted his palm to quieten her and stared in her eyes until she lowered her gaze.

"It's your first body, I understand, but a crime scene is sacred."

She nodded, shuffled her feet, her fingers linked, and did not raise her head.

"I'll not report the incident this time, and like I said, it won't happen again."

Darcy nodded. "No, it won't happen again."

"Now, go outside and talk to the workmen who found the body."

Albie watched her climb the stairs and glanced around the basement. Moss sprang from muddied walls and the smell of damp soil invaded his nose and assaulted the back of his throat. He breathed deeply and lifted his hands trying to still his shaking fingers. He patted his jacket pocket and felt for his cigarettes. But he resisted the urge to light one up and walked forward tentatively, one step at a time, while trying to breathe. Insipid thoughts invaded his mind, memories he'd buried as a child. He stumbled into the wall, and slid to the floor. He pressed his fingers to his temples but could not stave off the dread in his stomach or the thump in his head.

Powerless to shake the images dancing in his head, Albie's thoughts travelled to a time and place that seeped from locked memories. A place where he first experienced an utterly paralysing fear, a fear he'd never wanted to resurface. It had been the end of his childhood innocence. Albie sank back on his haunches. Damp and mildew cloyed his airways, and darkness poked at the back of his mind until he lifted his head.

Once again, he was back in the woods—a seven-year-old tearaway. It was 1973, and he was desperate for his father's attention.

Albie knelt on a blanket of damp leaves covering rain-drenched soil that soaked his knees. A brisk, frigid breeze whipped between the branches, undressing the trees of their last leaves and slapping any skin uncovered on his body. He jumped at the sound of a deep voice he would recognise anywhere. It covered a distance, carried on the wind from the thicket. He dared to inch around the thick, gnarled, moss-covered trunk—his only protection from the people on the other side.

"Gracie, you disappoint me. How many times? Never mind, betrayal knows no number."

The woman, hands and feet bound, coughed as he loosened her gag. She wriggled, reminding Albie of an eel before being beheaded and gutted.

The group of dark-clothed men surrounded her writhing body. One growled a warning, and the woman froze. Her muddied, off-white clothing further restricted her trussed-up body. To seven-year-old Albie, she resembled a caricature of a restrained mental patient—a familiar figure in the dark comic books Albie enjoyed reading. But this wasn't the scene from a comic book. This was real.

2

"Sir?" Albie felt a nudge on his shoulder and stretched his hand to steady himself. A concerned pair of blue eyes studied his face. "Are you okay?" Darcy asked, her voice hushed.

Albie glanced to either side, wiped dirty hands down the front of his jacket, straightened his tie, and smoothed his hair. He stood and brushed past Darcy without a word. He grabbed the partial bannister, and took the worn steps two at a time, not stopping until he'd reached the open back door.

Albie wiped sweat from his forehead and ran his finger inside his shirt collar. The heat was stifling. The temperature had peaked thirty degrees at the beginning of the month and looked set to continue. He emerged into what barely passed as a garden, stepped over a child's broken tricycle, and dodged a couple of dumped tyres half hidden by overgrown grass. The garden, like the rest of the house, was neglected. Albie stretched, reached inside his top pocket, and hunted for the packet of cigarettes he kept for emergencies. He balanced one between his lips, lit it, closed his eyes, and inhaled.

Over the fence at the end of the garden, a narrow, overgrown footpath separated a wooded area from the back of the property. It was alive with the sounds of birds, children's voices, and the occasional bark of a dog. Albie squinted and his hand shook as he shielded his eyes. In the heat, it was a hazy mirage, a product of the assault from the unyielding sun. He turned back towards the house. Since he'd left the building, more officers had arrived, and a search of the property had begun.

Albie ground the cigarette into the dirt, then lifted his foot and used a knot on the trunk of the heavily laden apple tree to raise him high enough to reach the lowest branch. As he climbed, the sickly scent of overripe fruit was nauseating. He edged his way towards the end of the branch until he'd perched on the top of the fence. Fruit fell to the ground as he leapt from the fence, and the branch snapped back.

Albie tumbled into an awkward forward roll, swearing as his back hit the solid dry earth. He struggled to his feet, flicking dust and debris from his suit and hair. He slipped off his jacket and draped it over the top of the fence. Sweating, he rolled up his sleeves, loosened his tie, and undid the top two buttons of his shirt.

He needed to focus—a young girl was missing, and others were turning up dead. Sian Wilkins deserved his full attention. He was going to find her and get the promotion he craved. Albie had his list of suspects. The list was a few pages long and consisted of some dubious characters.

One name kept his attention: Billy Stanton, a predator who preys on both women and children. Albie disliked him the first time they met.

It had only been two days before Sian went missing when the call of a disturbance came into the station.

"Darcy, we're up." Albie gulped the last mouthful of water before heading to the stairs hearing the hurried clip-clop of his colleague's heels following behind.

"Let me catch you up on this family." Albie said over the roof of the car as he opened the door and slid into the driver's seat.

Darcy nodded, Albie pulled out of the car park and headed towards the Fennick Estate.

"Angie Wilkinson, the tenant at the address, was driving a car involved in a crash that killed two people–her husband and baby son."

"That's awful...heartbreaking" Darcy gasped.

"As you can imagine, it's been traumatic for her and her daughters who were with their grandma at the time." He turned into the estate and slowed outside a squat brick semi-detached house.

Darcy looked around him at the ordinary house. "Quiet enough now."

"Yup, let's introduce you to Angie."

The front door flew open as Albie bent forward to unlatch the garden gate and a dishevelled man backed up the path. "And by the time I get back I expect you to have my money, slut."

Albie jogged up the path until he reached the man, and raised his hands, palms forward. "Woah, just a minute there."

"What the...shit. Which busybody called the pigs?"

"Calm down, Billy."

Billy shrugged and continued to the gate.

"That's officer Nicholls," Albie nodded at Darcy, "And she isn't going to move until I say you can go."

"Listen, I came for the money she owes me, that's all." He pointed at the door where a woman with a fragile build stood.

Albie turned his attention towards the woman standing on the doorstep. She looked more fragile than she had on his last visit to the house, if that was possible. "What's he been selling you this time, Angie?"

Angie's eyes flickered in Billy's direction and her body tensed. She cupped one hand over the other to hide her shaking. She lowered her head. "No DS Edwards, it's nothing like that. I...I owe him for babysitting and my benefits don't come till tomorrow."

Albie stared at one and then the other before strolling towards Angie. "Billy can go now, Nicholls." He slipped past Angie Wilkinson and into the yellow stained living room on the right. "We've had a noise complaint, Angie. You may as well come in and sit down."

Angie grumbled about her neighbours and settled into a worn armchair opposite a high-tech television.

"New?" Albie asked while Darcy closed the front door.

"Present. From the girl's nan and grandad."

They both sat on the edge of an old sofa to Angie's left. Albie glanced around the disrepair of the doors on the sideboard, paper hanging from two walls, the stained carpet, and torn curtains. He remembered the first time he visited Angie. An ambulance had dropped her home a month after the accident, and he helped her get settled. Everything had been immaculate and cherished. It was devastating the impact one mistake could have on the rest of your life.

"Are the girls home?"

Angie looked up from her clasped hands. "At school. I've

only just got them back from Social Services...please don't take them away. I couldn't bear–"

Albie rose from the sofa and took the few steps that separated them. He knelt before her and placed a hand over hers. "Shh, I'm not here to take the kids away, Angie. I'm here to make sure you're okay."

He noticed Darcy had stopped writing and was watching the interaction closely.

Angie pulled her hands from under Albie's. "That's not what you said when you arrived." Her blunt accusation made him step back.

"We have to follow up a complaint, but it was quiet when we arrived and the only person shouting around here was Billy Stanton."

Angie studied her hands again. "Billy's just helping me out."

"That's what worries me. Is he staying here?" Albie glanced around the room and spotted men's trainers and a sweatshirt too large to be Angie's.

"Not your business." She looked up but did not meet his eyes.

"Is he supplying you with drugs?"

Angie remained silent.

"Mum? We're home." A voice shouted from the back. "Can I make some toast? Sian's hungry."

"I'll make some in a minute. Come in here."

Angie went to the door and ushered the girls into the room. "These officers were just leaving."

Albie grinned. "Shelley. Sian. It's been a while. How's school?"

Shelley's face lit up. "It's good, thanks. Are you here to take us for a ride in the police car again?"

"Not today. But my workmate, Darcy, has been looking

forward to seeing your book collection and Sian's Barbie dolls."

Shelly's face lit up again and Sian hid behind her sister but couldn't hide the shy smile on her face.

Darcy knelt to Sian's height. "That's right, I've been excited to see your toys. Can you take me to your room?"

Shelley took Sian's hand and led the way. "Follow us," she said over her shoulder as they left the room.

Albie waited until he heard the thuds of the girl's steps overhead before he spoke again. "You realise Billy Stanton is the wrong man to help you out, right?"

Angie bit down hard on her lip and fisted her hands in her lap before answering. "Billy is the only person who has offered to help me out and I appreciate his help. I didn't see you lot when I was struggling to feed the kids."

"You had my number. I told you to call anytime–"

"And take my kids away? That's what happened last time." Angie pulled a tissue from under her bra strap and dabbed a few tears from under her eyes.

Albie rubbed his fingers back and forth across his forehead. "You'd been using drugs…you were unconscious when the kids got home…they had to go into care until you were better. Don't you see, Billy is the type of guy who'll get you using again."

Angie sprang from her chair and opened the door. "Okay, you've had your say, now it's time you and the other officer left."

With a slow shake of his head, Albie stood and made for the door. He stopped in front of her and placed his hand on her shoulder. "Get rid of Billy; he's a leech. And don't leave him alone with the girls again–rumour has it that he prefers young girls to women his own age."

Angie's face paled and she gasped.

After calling Darcy, he left the house knowing he'd done all he could to warn Angie.

Two days later Sian had been reported missing and Albie cursed himself for not kicking up more of a fuss.

On the other side of the footpath, under the canopy of the trees, the undergrowth rustled, probably a small animal using the foliage as cover from the heat of the day. The shrill sounds of children's laughter rang out in the distance–carefree and exhilarating. It reminded him of local woods he used to play in when he was a child.

Albie leaned against a tree and with the back of his hand, wiped the sweat from his forehead. It had been eight days since Sian had gone missing. The local community had all rallied around and searched for the seven-year-old, the public's fear ignited. Sian had disappeared from her bed and had been taken through her open bedroom window. The frenzy began with a headline: *Snatched While She Slept*.

When Albie had visited his mother, at the beginning of the investigation, she had grabbed his hand between hers and said, 'You must find her, Albie. No seven-year-old should be exposed to violence.' The fear in her voice was the echo of a nation.

3

———————

"DS Edwards?"

Albie drew himself to standing, brushed his fingers through his hair, and cleared his throat before attempting to answer. "Over here."

He watched as his colleague followed the trail towards him and knew he wasn't much support. It was Darcy's third day on the job and her first case. So far, Nicholls had been as efficient as she could be, all things considered. In fact, he wondered how she was still functioning. This was the first time today she'd shown nervousness, and then she'd asked that bloody stupid question as if he'd want to share the experience of seeing his first dead body with her. Now he was struggling to stay in the present. But then again, how was Nicholls to know he'd seen his first dead body at the same age of the poor, innocent girl? And not just a dead body, but the body of a murder victim?

"They've finished in the basement, sir. Body's being removed, and Mr. Nico said he will see you later for an update. He suggested that I'm more careful around his crime scene in future."

Albie stifled a grin and shook his head.

"Take no notice of Leo. He's a sarcastic bastard when he wants to be." He stepped back into the narrow lane that edged the gardens and walked towards the fence.

"Right. We need to get back to the station and share the information." He took his jacket from the fence, hunted through his trouser pockets for the car keys. Albie turned and strolled towards the road at the end of the lane. He nodded in the direction of a coffee shop over the road and held out a ten-pound note. "I'll have a cappuccino with two sugars and a croissant. Get yourself something. I'll meet you at the car and I might even let you drive."

As he reached the car and slid into the passenger seat, his words reminded him of the evening of his seventh birthday when he was desperate to see his father.

"I'll meet you at the car," his father had shouted to Jerry as he pulled the collar of his thick black coat up against the icy wind.

Jerry the Giant. That was Albie's nickname for his father's scary friend. It was a secret he'd never share with anyone else. In fact, Albie often hid from the man whenever he entered a room. Just his presence made him sweat and shake; it even made him breathless.

Jerry worked closely with his father, Freddie, and drove him to business meetings. As far as Albie remembered, Freddie had never driven the shiny black Rover. Albie had only travelled in the Rover once, but he'd never forgotten the soft cream seats, cool to the touch, the purr of the engine, and the polished walnut dashboard. Mellow music escaped from the radio, and he'd smiled up at his father while he tapped his fingers on the armrest and hummed out of tune. And like Freddie, Albie knew he would work hard to be the owner of a sleek black Rover.

A chill wind whipped leaves in a crazy dance, unable to settle, unable to rest. Albie's insides felt the same as he ducked down on the pavement, huddled next to the rear of the car. He edged out with caution. Anger fueled him as he recalled parts of a conversation he'd overheard that evening so long ago. He'd been so excited to see his uncle, especially when he handed him a hastily wrapped gift. Lego. He'd run to the other room, opened the box, and tipped the contents over the carpet.

"Are you crazy, woman? What would possess you to even get in touch with that monster?" Albie stopped fiddling with the bricks he'd clipped together, placed them back on the carpet, and crept into the hallway. Careful to avoid the creaky boards, he pressed his back flat to the wall and edged as close to the living room door as he dared.

"Shh, Albie doesn't need to hear this. And whatever you think about Freddie, he's still Albie's father."

"Oh right, 'shh', that's your answer for everything, isn't it?" Albie's uncle raised his voice before adding, "Wouldn't want the boy to find out what a bastard his father is, would we?"

Albie clamped his hand over his mouth, and he slowed his breath. Each one echoed in his head, and he was sure it would only be moments before they discovered him.

"He's seven, Morgan. All he really wants for his birthday is to spend time with Freddie. I just..."

"You just what, Marianne? You just forgot about all the times I was called to the hospital? The times I nursed you back from near death?" His voice lowered and Albie had to strain to catch the next words his mother whimpered, "Funnily, I don't give a shit if Freddie's his biological dad. He lost his right to have anything to do with this family when he used my sister as a punchbag."

Albie slid along the wall. He felt a sudden need to go back and build Lego bricks into towers.

"It doesn't matter, anyway. You got your wish. Freddie Hurst

is too busy to even spare an hour with his son. You can tell Albie. It's going to break his heart."

The pain began as a small hard bud in the pit of Albie's stomach. He realised he wouldn't see his dad, not even on his birthday. But as the day progressed, the bud, fed by sadness, his mother's false smiles, and his uncle's lack of eye contact, had bloomed. A beautiful red anger, protected by an impressive stem covered in poisonous thorns. It threatened to devour his innocent love for his father. He'd decided, used his lie, and got out of the house on the pretence of visiting his friend next door. Instead, he walked to his father's work and waited to see him.

Albie watched as Jerry strolled past to the car in front, bent down, and chatted with the driver. Keeping crouched, Albie waddled to the back passenger door, took a breath, pushed in the button, and eased the door open, expecting to be shouted at or grabbed at any second. The street was bustling with the weekend frivolity of thrill seekers and their raucous laughter, and each so engrossed in themselves that Albie's actions went unnoticed.

He pulled the door until he heard a click and sat still, listening to his pounding heart until the beats evened out and quietened. From the back footwell of the darkened car, Albie scanned the back seat for the best hiding place. His throat tightened as he assessed a few options in the oppressive space, the need to see his father stronger than his growing sense of regret. Thoughts flitted through his mind as if carried on the wings of butterflies. What if he's caught? How could he explain being in the car? What's the worst that could happen? With a hesitant sigh, Albie slid into the opposite footwell, curled into a ball, and dragged a musky blanket from the back seat.

"Jerry, we're dropping Gracie off on the way." His father's voice was loud and urgent outside the car. Albie shuffled his position and pulled the blanket over his head. The noise of the

revellers was muffled and distant, but his father's authoritative voice was unmistakable. "Now, Jerry."

Doors opened.

"You don't have to do this, Mr Hurst. The bus stop's just in the next street." Albie stilled at the sound of the woman's disjointed pitch. It reminded him of a frog's squeal when his cat played with it at the end of the garden. He'd often wondered why it tortured the animal rather than just kill its prey.

"No problem," Freddie answered as he slid into the seat beside her. He cleared his throat, stared straight ahead as Jerry indicated, and joined a steady stream of traffic.

Albie opened a gap in the blanket when he heard someone shuffle across the back seat until the woman's body pressed tight to the other door. He held in a cry as the pointed heel of her shoe stamped down on his hand. He thought she'd spotted him moving under the blanket for a moment. She stared in his direction, then shrugged her shoulders, and shifted her feet so her legs angled towards Freddie.

The woman wiped the sweat from her brow, even though the temperature was a low single figure. Freddie leaned in close to the woman and reached out. She stilled as he ran his fingers down the side of her face—a tender motion. Albie had seen Freddie do that to his mum before.

"Relax, Gracie," Freddie whispered, and the woman edged into his side. Like a magnetic attraction they'd learnt about at school. Albie tried to close his eyes to his father's action but couldn't move. He lay in the footwell and peeked from below the blanket. He watched as Freddie's fingers lingered around the base of the woman's neck. In a single movement, Freddie straddled her. His hands tightened around her neck, that reddened as he pressed both thumbs into her skin just above her collarbone, and she shrunk back into the leather seat. The woman struggled against his hold. She pushed her heels into the floor and pushed back

further, higher, trying to escape his clawed fingers. He pinioned her between the grip of his boney thighs, and she was going nowhere.

"I wouldn't struggle." Freddie hissed. A whimper escaped her mouth. "Now, now." He wiped a hand across her face. Snot and saliva crossed her cheek to her temple before mingling with her hairline.

"Please, Mr Hurst." She sniffled. Her voice cracked, "I don't understand. I've–"

"Shh," he curled his fingers into her hair, twisted it into a fist, and tugged. "It's probably best to listen, don't you think?"

The woman gasped as his grip tightened. Tears streamed down her face as he forced her to face his sneers. His face contorted as he leaned in his voice gruff. "I hear you've been disloyal to me, Gracie. Not the angel I thought you were. Pillow talk… It'll get you into all sorts of trouble."

"I. Listen, I don't–"

He released her hair, cupped his hand, covered her trembling mouth, and pressed down.

With a slow shake of the head, Freddie continued. "Too late, my angel. We'll be there soon, and you can confess. You can clear your conscience."

Jerry slowed the car and veered off the road onto an unlit track. The full moon, partially covered by low grey clouds, tormented them the further they travelled into the darkness.

4

———————

Shelley grabbed hold of her little sister's hand and lifted one strap of her hold-all over her shoulder as they reached the roadside. She looked both ways before hurrying Sian across to the other side. Sian had been unusually quiet since they left their mum asleep on the couch. Still holding hands, Shelley swung their arms back and forth skipping towards the park gates. Sian smiled for the first time and ran to keep up.

The park was quiet, only a few dog walkers and a jogger who headed towards the gates opposite. The play area was deserted. It was lunchtime so everyone else would be at home eating and they could have the whole park to themselves.

"Come on, beat you to the swings." Shelley let go of Sian's hand and pretended to race her into the play area.

"Wait, that's not fair, you are bigger than me, stop." Sian whined. "That's my favourite swing." Her shoulders rounded, her lips pouted, and she looked up between slit eyes.

"Aw, don't be a baby, Sian. I saved it for you." Shelley

pushed her legs back one last time and jumped off as she swung forward. "What's wrong with you today, anyway?"

"Nothing."

Sian climbed onto the seat. "Push me." She shouted, pumping her legs backwards and forwards as fast as she could.

"Only if you tell me why you've been so quiet. What's got you so moody?"

Sian shook her head. "I can't tell."

Shelly watched her little sister use one hand to pretend to zip her lips together, turn a lock and throw away an imaginary key. A chill ran down her spine and she shuddered at the action she herself had been taught to ensure her silence.

"You can tell me, we're sisters–sisters don't keep secrets from each other–sisters share everything."

Sian had stopped swinging. Her eyes wide in her elf-like face, tears rolled down her cheeks and she shook her head. "I can't...he'll hurt you and Mummy."

Shelly took her sister's hand and guided her towards a wooden bench. She pulled Sian towards her side and cuddled her.

The thought of Billy touching Sian sent waves of nausea to the back of her throat. One deep breath...two ...by the third she put a barrier between her thoughts and memories. She stroked the back of Sian's hand lightly with her fingers.

"Shh," she whispered into Sian's soft mousey hair. "He's not going to touch you because he's not going to know where you are." She smoothed her hand over her sister's hair and slipped a finger under her chin lifting her face until she met her eyes. "We're going to play a game of hide 'n' seek."

A nervous grin flicked on her delicate face for a second. "I'm scared."

"That's why we're not going home until Billy's gone."

"But Billy's mum's friend." The exasperated sound of her delicate voice matched her wide-eyed stare framed by arched eyebrows.

"Don't worry, I'll talk to Mum, I'll make her understand." Standing, Shelley held out her hand. "I'll sort it, promise. Come on."

With Sian's hand wrapped in her own, Shelley nodded towards the woods and led the way.

The white house stood on the opposite side of a clearing at the edge of the woods.

"Look, over there." Shelley pointed to the boarded-up house and rubbed Sian's shoulder. Told you we'd find it!"

Sian had scrambled to keep up with Shelley's stride–her little legs tiring. Sian was too heavy to carry, so Shelley had to slow the pace down to stop Sian's whining and thankfully it had worked.

"It's not white."

With a forced grin, Shelley grabbed her sister's hand and led her round the back of the building.

"You're right, it's not. And it probably hasn't been white for years." She leant on a window and pried back an unfastened slat of wood then faced Sian. "But one thing I do know–it's a safe place to hide. Come on!"

An abandoned milk crate stood nearby. Shelley dragged it beneath the gap she'd made in the window. She threw her holdall into the house then stood on the top and used her arms to hoist her slim body onto the windowsill. She sat in silence and listened for a moment. When she was sure they were alone, she leaned out of the window. "Sian, it's okay.

Can you climb onto the crate? I'll be able to lift you through the gap, but you have to stand on the crate."

Shelley watched as her sister hesitated and peered over her shoulder.

'The quicker you do this the sooner we hide. He won't find us here. I promise." She leaned further out of the window and held her arms out for Sian to grab.

"Cor, you're heavier than I thought."

Sian giggled; it was the first real reaction Shelley had heard from her all day. Sian was normally voracious for life. Plastering a smile on her own face, to stave off tears, she held her sister's hand.

"This way."

They stayed on the ground floor, their footsteps echoed across the floorboards of a spacious room. Probably once the living room, but difficult to identify in the bleak darkness of the place.

"Quickly!"

Doubt entered her mind, along with it, fear. Shelley hurried them down a narrow corridor, regularly glancing over her shoulder. Would they be discovered? Is this the right thing to do? She only knew that she had to protect her sister.

They entered another room. A kitchen island dominated the area and was surrounded with old-fashioned kitchen appliances and wrecked kitchen cupboards. On the opposite side to the boarded up back door were a couple of concrete steps leading to a cellar.

"Nearly there. Behind the small door is a crawl space." Shelley edged some empty crates to one side and bent down. "In here." She held out her hand, but Sian stood frozen to the spot.

"I can't..."

"Yes, you can. This is a safe place." She shuffled back and cuddled her frightened sister into a tight hug. "Listen to me. If we go home, Billy is going to hurt you, Sian...really hurt you. Here, you're safe. I'm with you. And I bet you can't guess what I've got in my bag!"

Sian looked up with a smile. "Tigger?"

"Even better, Tigger and a picnic! Let's go inside and share our picnic with Tigger."

Shelley, seeing her sister enjoy the picnic, knew everything was going to work out. All she had to do was wait for Sian to fall asleep with Tigger and then she'd go to her mum for help. Mum would take their side against Billy, and it would be just the three of them again.

5

———————

"Edwards, we're approaching the station." Darcy's voice and the jolt of his stomach as they tackled the speed bumps woke him from an unintentional nap.

"Watch it." Leaning forward, he reached out and grabbed the dashboard. "You're supposed to brake before you take the corner."

"Ha, ha, hilarious. There's nothing wrong with my driving. You're just in shock because I had to wake you up."

"I wasn't asleep. Just resting my eyes. I thought I was in capable hands. Obviously mistaken."

She reversed into a tight space between two badly parked cars. Albie grinned and shook his head before squeezing out of the acute gap, in an effort not to scrape the door of the car in the next parking bay.

"Here." She threw the keys over the car's roof, and he caught them between his fingers. "You can drive in the future." She strode towards the front of the building.

"Oh, come on," he shouted after her, "I was only messing with you. Nicholls, wait, will you?" Albie jogged to catch up.

He reached in his pocket, the need for a smoke increasing. He tapped the cigarette box but resisted the temptation to leave Darcy to her sulk.

As he turned the corner, he spotted her slim frame, back against the wall, standing on one leg, the other bent, foot supported by the wall, her head in her hands. Albie shuffled, raised his hand about to comfort her, then thought better and cleared his throat.

She sniffed and looked his way before pulling out a tissue to dab her eyes.

"I didn't mean anything by it, you know, you're driving."

He looked at his shoes and noticed scuff marks that weren't there earlier. "It was supposed to be a joke."

Darcy spluttered a laugh, blew her nose, raised her lightly blotched face to his, and smiled.

"I'm not that delicate, sir. It's just, well, it's been quite a shock for me today. My first experience with a dead body, and it's a child." Her voice cracked, and she took a few deep breaths before continuing. "I messed up. Knocked equipment over, probably contaminated a crime scene, and then made you angry. All in all, it's a day I'd like to end now."

Albie studied her face for a moment. He couldn't disagree that she hadn't had the best day. Sometimes the truth mattered, but not today.

"Listen, so today was a bad day. After two weeks with the team, your first murder case, it could have been worse." He strolled toward the main entrance. "Come on. You don't want to finish the day being late for the briefing."

She pushed herself off the wall, straightened her uniform, licked a new tissue, and wiped the mascara from under her eyes before smoothing down her hair and making a mental note to visit the toilets at the first opportunity.

"You still said nothing about what I did to anger you

earlier." She watched as he flexed his jaw and his shoulders stiffened. "I just thought if I knew what I'd done, I'd be less likely to make the same mistake again."

Albie stopped and held her upper arm. The momentum spun her around, her eyes wide.

"PC Nicholls, if we're going to work together, I'll not make excuses for my behaviour. Let's just say you asked a question and it hit a nerve. Now I'm going to get us both a drink. I suggest you wash your face. I'll meet you in the incident room. Tomorrow is a new day. We'll start afresh." He spun away and jogged into the building.

In the incident room, he handed a drink and a cheese and pickle sandwich to a fresher-faced Darcy.

"How did you guess?" She lifted the sandwich in appreciation. "I suppose my grumbling stomach gave me away."

Albie nodded, but his attention was drawn to DS Rachel Fawn. She strode towards him with a look of determination in her round eyes; unapologetic to those she elbowed to get to him.

"Bit of a ball's up at the crime scene, I heard, Acting DS Edwards." The semblance of a grin grazed her lips, and her emphasis on 'acting' was unmistakable. Albie searched her eyes and waited for her to continue. He wondered what was going on in his colleague's conniving mind.

He knew Rachel Fawn had her eye on usurping his throne. Knowing the Detective Sergeant's position wasn't his yet, he remained cagey, and he sipped his drink before speaking.

"So, Fawn, did you arrest that flasher on the estate today?"

She grinned an all-knowing smile. "You'll find out soon enough. Let's just say it's good one of us knows our arse from our armpit." She winked at him before heading back towards her group of cronies at the front of the room.

"What's she got to be so pleased about? Didn't we find a dead child today?" Darcy asked.

Albie shrugged and took another swallow of his Coke, which was now lukewarm and flat. He followed the swing of Fawn's hips, as purposeful and triumphant as her speech. At that moment, Albie knew, as a colleague, she would always be an enemy. Professional jealousy, he could deal with, but this was deeper. Rachel Fawn saw beneath his facade. The mask of indifference, prepared daily and worn like war paint. If she peeled it away, it would expose a father's son. Despite his denial, Fawn made him nervous.

"Afternoon, team. Just a quick update." DI Sarah Masters scanned the room until her eyes reached Albie, where she settled. "You'll be pleased to hear—we're near to arrests. I say arrests with trepidation. It appears we may have stumbled across a paedophile ring."

Albie cleared his throat and lowered his head, uncomfortable with the DI's stare. How had this happened without his knowledge? Wasn't he supposed to be Acting DS? Yet Rachel Fawn knew enough to taunt him before the briefing. He shook his head, bewildered. Could this day get any worse?

"... so, keep up the good work. We need you to be vigilant and follow every lead from the public. There are witnesses on the estate who are oblivious to what they've seen. Let's jog a few memories, shall we? DS Edwards, a word, please."

Albie walked towards Masters, ignoring the stares from colleagues, and avoiding eye contact, especially with Darcy.

Masters walked through the double doors that led into a narrow corridor painted industrial magnolia with hard-wearing brown cord carpet. Apart from name plaques next to the doors of the offices, the walls were nondescript.

"Whatever issues you and Fawn have need to be put aside." Masters raised a hand before he could object and continued, "The thing is, your investigating styles are so different they complement each other. Your priority must be finding Sian Wilkinson. Fawn did some digging into step-dad's background, and that's how she found links with the paedophile ring. You see, Billy Stanton's done this before, wriggled his way into the life of a vulnerable mother to take advantage of her kids."

"And the dead girl?"

"Fawn can follow up on the dead girl and see if we can link her to Wilkins. Your focus must be Sian. There was a sighting of a young girl of a similar description alone in Falcon woods called in by a local dog walker." She handed a piece of paper to Albie. "A good enough place to start, don't you think?"

Albie nodded and took the paper from her hand. "So, what's happening about the paedophile gang?"

"Leave it to Fawn. The investigation is still in its infancy. She's contacted relevant teams across the force. Your job is to find Sian alive."

6

———

Darcy smiled at Ms Ryan and thanked her before flipping her notebook closed. The photo of Sian hadn't helped.

"Could be her but wouldn't want to commit. She was filthy like she'd rolled in dirt; it was all over her skin, and even her hair was more of a dirty blonde."

"Anything else you can remember? Did you hear her voice?"

Ms Ryan slid her glasses up her nose and stared into the distance. A black Labrador lay next to her. Saliva dribbled from his mouth, his fur slick from a recent shower, and he panted in a frantic rhythm.

"No," she shook her head as she spoke. "I can't say I heard her speak, but she did put her finger to her lips. I knew she was scared. Her eyes were wide, and her hands shook. It gave me the heebie-jeebies; I can tell you. Felt like we were being watched."

Albie stood and listened. Darcy had taken control of the conversation and wasn't doing a bad job.

"What happened next?"

The woman bent and trailed her fingers over the dog's wet fur. "Well, I was unsure of what to do next. I made a move towards her, but she panicked and moved further away. I didn't want her distressed, so I whispered I'd get help."

"Okay, is that when you phoned the station?"

She bent her head and studied her fingernails, which were neatly manicured, painted a pale pink, and appeared to be momentarily more interesting than their conversation.

Albie cleared his throat. He'd always felt long silences a waste of time, and in this case, precious minutes were wasted when they could be searching for Sian. The sky darkened, and a rumble drifted in the distance.

Ms Ryan's eyes met Albie's frustrated frown, and she continued so quickly the words tripped over each other as they left her mouth. "I didn't... couldn't... not straight away, no mobile pho—"

"Wait," Albie interrupted, "so where were you when you contacted the police?"

The woman's eyes widened at his urgency. "I had to walk home to–"

"So, there was no one else around, someone with a phone, someone else who could have phoned immediately?"

"I just, I didn't think. I wasn't sure what to do. She was so scared. What if I'd asked someone dangerous?"

Albie paced, pulled his phone from his trouser pocket, and spoke into it in hurried whispers.

"How far are the woods from here by foot?" He cupped his hand over the phone as he directed the question to the woman, who was in the middle of justifying her actions to Darcy.

"About twenty minutes at a quick pace. I can point you

in the right direction." She talked Darcy through the quickest route.

"Oh, no, you don't," Albie hung up his phone and strode towards them, "You'll do more than that, Ms Ryan." He looked up at the sky as lightning struck overhead and counted to twenty in his head before the rumble of thunder followed. "Grab your raincoat and the dog's lead. You're showing us exactly where you last saw the girl." Turning his attention to Darcy he said, "The team are on their way, a storms on our tail, and we need to collect as much evidence as we can before it's washed away."

An eerie silence greeted them the further they ventured into the woods. Dusk accompanied the silence, and with the dark skies and closely knit trees, the tension and urgency for the situation enveloped the trio. Ms Ryan trembled as they moved towards a roar of thunder, and her dog whimpered when lightning cracked the sky and lit up the canopy over their heads.

"Look, isn't this dangerous?" Stopping, she shivered as rain fell from the sky.

Albie ushered her forward, but Darcy rested a hand on his arm. "Perhaps Ms Ryan can point us in the right direction. Where did you last see her?"

She pointed further into the wood. Albie barged between the two women and jogged in the general direction. "When you reach a fallen tree that cuts off the path, turn right. That's where I saw her, but whether she's still there..." She shrugged, knelt by the dog, and whispered in its ear while stroking its wet coat.

Albie moved deeper into the woods, slipping on rain-drenched clumps of grass. "Nicholls, follow me. Ms Ryan can go," he shouted over his shoulder. The rain was much needed after the heatwave, but all Albie was concerned about was it destroying evidence. He gasped for air as he ran–he just needed to keep moving.

"Over here, Nicholls. Ring it in. We need an ambulance."

Albie leaned over the still form, his fingers wrapped around her wrist, searching for a pulse, her hand white and limp. He bent his head, put his ear against her mouth, then smiled at Nicholls.

"She's breathing. Shallow breaths, but she's breathing."

He blew out a breath, hands on hips and smiled at Darcy, who smiled back. Albie watched as she bent forward, with her hands on her knees, and concentrated on slowing her breath.

Sirens blared in the background, and Albie nodded in the noise's direction. He stepped closer to the girl and glanced down at a nasty gash to the side of her head. A small pool of dark blood formed from the trickle escaping the wound.

"That's Shelley?" Darcy said, bringing her hands to her face, and exhaling in what Albie thought was relief.

Albie nodded in reply as he focused once more on the injured girl by his feet.

"Where's Sian?"

Darcy spun in every direction, before bending her legs and leaning over, sticking her head between her knees. Paramedics ran into the clearing, escorted by members of the team, and Albie made space for them to work.

A small grumble of thunder mumbled on a light breeze followed by a feeble slash of lightning. The rain picked up again, and Albie sat on a cut-down tree trunk. He looked towards the figure on the ground, and his heart rate sped up as she opened her eyes and returned his stare.

The woman in white had stared at him from where she lay,

He peered into the pleading eyes of a beautiful woman who looked like an angel, dressed in white laying in a pool of blood. Her hand was outstretched in his direction. A man stood over her, his face deadpan. A knife held loosely by his side dripped blood while he stared at her pale fingers.

An innate instinct to survive took over. Albie trembled, kneeling in the undergrowth, stock still, afraid to react. Even at seven, Albie realised he'd seen too much. He was sure the dream-like situation could be explained, he was sure. But he was not sure enough to make his presence known. He kept his eyes focused on his shaking hands and unstuck his dry tongue from the roof of his mouth, then tried to swallow.

Pain nibbled at his bare legs, from a patch of stinging nettles and bramble scratches. He so wanted to drag his nails over the irritation. Instead, he raised his head in time to see the woman lifted from the muddy ground. The man with the knife held her like a husband carrying his wife over the threshold. He watched them go further into the woods; the woman was limp. Her head rocked to the rhythm of his movements. Albie could almost believe she was asleep but for the fear in her wide eyes.

"Edwards, can you hear me? Shelley will survive." Fawn squatted in front of Albie and studied his face. "A shock, I know, but Shelley mentioned Sian."

Albie wiped his arm across his forehead. He ignored her and walked towards Darcy, placed an arm around her, and helped her to stand.

"Are you okay? According to Fawn, Shelley mentioned Sian."

Darcy smiled, straightened, and eased her arm from his grip.

"She's still out there. We've work to do." Albie said and headed towards the ambulance.

The doors of the ambulance were fully open. The internal lights mimicked spotlights on a stage—the principal actors fully focused on the performances they undertook.

"How's she doing?"

One paramedic looked over his shoulder while fiddling with a drip. "The injury's nasty, but she's gained consciousness. A few stitches should be enough."

"Don't suppose there's any chance I can ask a couple of questions now?"

The paramedic shook his head. "No mate, our jobs to patch her up and deliver–"

"I know," Albie said as he reached for his warrant card. "Thing is, her sister is missing. Can you give us five?" Albie stepped onto the platform and glanced at the second paramedic as she jotted information on a form before checking Shelley's vitals.

The first paramedic spoke, "We're off in three minutes, mate."

Albie sat in the cushioned chair at the side of the bed. "Hi, Shelley. I'm Albie, you might remember I visited your house with Darcy?"

Shelley's eyes opened wide, and she spoke, her voice hoarse. Albie leaned closer and just caught a whisper, "Darcy..."

He gestured towards Darcy to join them. "Darcy is here, Shelley."

Darcy squeezed into the gap between Albie and the patient. She steadied Shelley's shaking hand by wrapping it in her own. "It's okay, Shelley. Where's Sian? If you have any idea where she is, you can tell us."

Shelley leaned towards Darcy, who patted her hand. "I hid her." Darcy stiffened.

Albie nodded to his colleague to continue with her questions. "It's okay, Shelley. Where did you hide Sian?"

Tears trailed down her muddied face. "I had to hide her from him. She was next. He was coming for her next."

Albie grimaced at Shelley's answers, his fists clenched. As Darcy continued to reassure the girl, she wiped Shelley's hair back from her face and dabbed her tears with a tissue. "It's okay, honey. You did what you thought was right. Help us find Sian. Where is she hidden?"

"In the basement of the white house on the other side of the woods."

Albie jumped out of the back of the ambulance just as the paramedic started the engine.

"We'll find her, Shelley. Dry your eyes. I'll see you soon."

"The white house?" Darcy asked Albie as she jumped from the back of the ambulance and faced him.

The ambulance drove slowly along the narrow pathway towards the main road while Albie jogged further into the woods with Darcy keeping pace. "It's a derelict house just on the other side of the woods." They ran on in silence, each of them concentrating on keeping their footing.

They ran into a clearing; Albie stopped and scanned the area to get his bearings. Darcy held her side for a moment until Albie nodded ahead.

"I've rung ahead. The team searching the woods should be at the house now." He started a slow jog as they raked the horizon for the silhouette of a dilapidated mansion not yet in view.

"What are we going to find? Eight days. What about food and water?" Darcy shouted. Albie shuddered at the thought then shook it off refusing to think the worst. They jogged and stumbled their way forward, the light fading fast.

The ringtone of his phone brought Albie to a standstill.

He bent forward as he answered, relieved to have a breather. He listened.

"We're five minutes away. Check the basement."

Neither spoke as they picked up the rhythm they'd had before and headed towards the building.

7

Fawn met them on the worn stone steps leading to the double doors, which lay open and guarded. Albie and Darcy followed. The beams of their flashlights bounced just a few feet ahead, enough to navigate the steep descent into the basement. A stench of waste hung in the air, and the taste embedded in the back of their throats. A dark underground world, the home of rodents that squealed as they scurried to avoid the intruders. Slimy residue covered the walls, while nature of a darker persuasion hung from the corners. Maggots fed on a crusty, yellow substance that climbed the rotten wooden skirting. Albie lifted his hand to his mouth to fend off a pungent smell of rot.

They came to a solid, locked door that had a pet entrance at its base.

"So, do we know if Sian is in there? Can you locate her position?"

Fawn answered for the PC guarding the door. "It's unclear. We've heard no sounds from the room, sir."

"Well, Rachel," Albie hid a grin; there would be time

enough to revel in the respect she'd just shown, "there's only one way to find out." He nodded towards the door.

Albie lowered his chest to the rough concrete ground, trying to ignore the damp absorbed through the front of his shirt as he gagged on the rancid stink. Angling the beam of his flashlight through the pet door, he scanned the internal room. An eerie silence hung heavy in the gloom of the abandoned space. Faint outlines of dumped, damaged, and unwanted objects, no longer useful, forgotten, and left to disintegrate. He strained his eyes, desperate to identify Sian's presence.

Albie hoped Darcy didn't suffer from claustrophobia.

"I know it's tight, Nicholls, but do you think you can wriggle through?"

Albie knelt on the jagged concrete that dug into his knees and heard Darcy wince when she knelt beside him. He shuffled back giving her room to manoeuvre.

Darcy dragged herself forward, grazed her fingers around the splintered edge of the small door, and inspected the wood for jagged edges.

Darcy turned to face him and nodded. "I'll give it a go."

Thin lines at the top of her nose and a furrow to her brow were the only signs of emotion he could spot as he studied her expression. She was their best bet, her slim physique an attribute.

"Keep talking to us."

She stretched her arms overhead and snaked her limbs and head through the creaking, flap of a door.

"You're doing great, Nicholls. If you can shimmy from side to side, your shoulders should go through at an angle. Left, that's it, slightly more to your left."

Wood splintered and stabbed into her upper torso as she angled her body to disengage her wedged shoulders. With each twist she winced. Once through, He saw Darcy drag herself forward commando style.

She scanned the semi-circle area with her flashlight. Just on the outskirts of the beam, a dark bundle squirmed—a subtle movement.

"Sian, it's okay. I'm here to help you. Don't be scared."

"Approach slowly. No unexpected movements. She'll be frightened, so it's important you keep her calm. Medical help will be here shortly." Albie whispered encouragement. "You can do this, Darcy. Let's get this little girl back to her mum, shall we?"

Albie watched as Darcy tried to stand upright, but the low ceiling kept her on her knees. Instead, she crawled towards the bundle at the back of the room. She continued to a corner, angling her body to manoeuvre next to the girl. Albie could see Sian's tiny heart-shaped face under a dirty navy hoodie that swamped her frail body. He wasn't sure if her lips were blue, but he was relieved when he heard Darcy tell the girl she was safe now.

Curled in a foetal position, the girl's grubby hand slumped on an empty water bottle. Her eyes were closed as if in sleep, and her blonde hair clung to her scalp in dirty curls. Crisp packets, chocolate bar wrappers, and a sandwich carton surrounded her like the remains of offerings. At least she'd had some food.

"Is there a pulse?" Albie asked, trying to keep the urgency from his voice. Darcy leaned forward and circled Sian's wrist with her fingers, searching for a sign of life. She smiled as a faint beat pulsed.

"There's a pulse, but it's slight. Where's that medical help?"

"We're on it, Nicholls. Comfort Sian. It's going to be loud. Wrap her in this." Albie shoved a blanket through the wooden hole in the door and wondered how she'd wriggled through such a tight gap.

He watched as Darcy wrapped the tiny body, then lay next to Sian on the ground. Her fingertips gently stroked the child's hair while the deafening noise of a battering ram held by two officers pounded the door, echoing around the space. The booming thuds sent bone-crunching vibrations through the claustrophobic space.

When the door finally gave, Sian opened her eyes, and blinked against the light. The water bottle she'd clung to dropped to the floor as she reached for Darcy and drew her closer.

"What is it, Sian?"

"Billy."

"What about, Billy? Does he know you're here?"

Sian whispered "No," then closed her eyes, her arm hung loose and her whole body went limp.

8

___

An owl's warning hoots carried on the breeze as they navigated their way back through the dark-ened wood in silence. Albie frowned as he assessed his colleague's filthy appearance in contrast with the massive grin lighting her dirt-streaked face.

"Well done, Darcy. You saved a young life today." They were all relieved when the paramedics announced Sian was stable after working on her for thirty minutes. He took one more draw on the cigarette, dropped the butt, and ground it into the mud. "This is the last packet I'm having."

The rain had eased to a fine drizzle by the time they reached the car outside Ms Ryan's house. Albie stared up at the windows as he guided Darcy to the passenger side of the car.

"You've done enough for one day." It wasn't until they'd both collapsed onto the seat that he spotted a movement in the upstairs curtain. Tempted to wave, instead, he started the car and pressed the horn as they left the curb.

He smiled at Darcy's obvious shock. "What?" He shrugged, a huge smile spread across his face. "Well, she

40

was a selfish cow. More concerned about herself than helping Shelley. We'd have found Sian hours ago if it wasn't for little miss self-indulgent."

The pubs they passed were full of customers, some overflowing to outside tables in the evening heat. A slight dip in temperature didn't seem to bother them. If anything, the storm had barely cleared the air. The noise and lights from the windows, streetlamps, and passing cars brought a crazy kind of calm to the car after the desolation and darkness of the White House.

"Home, or are you up for one more stop?"

Darcy lifted her face to meet his and he noted the dark circles under her tired eyes. "One stop where?"

"We need to talk to Shelley–"

"Now? She's been through a horrific experience, and she's scared."

In one movement, Albie took a gentle hold on the top of Darcy's arms. He frowned as he spoke, his concern obvious. "You're right, she's frightened for her sister and scared of Billy Stanton. Are we going to speak to her now or let Angie take her home to Billy?" A long silence between the two, then Albie added, "Not all decisions we make as police officers are cut and dry. Unfortunately, most land in a grey area and don't always benefit the victims. It sucks but our hands are tied."

They strolled into reception and showed their ID before being given the ward name where Shelley had a bed for the night.

"Up the stairs, second door on the right." The receptionist said.

The double doors opened onto a busy ward. The only nurse at the nurse's station was animated while speaking on the telephone. She smiled but held up a finger for them to wait. Albie turned his back to her and scanned his surroundings. Patients sat in the beds or on wooden chairs while others took cautious steps, holding tightly onto their IV poles.

"It's not quite visiting time yet. Why don't you have a coffee–"

Albie's attention went back to the nurse, he smiled at her and held up his warrant card.

"We need to ask Shelley Wilkinson. If you can guide us in the right direction?"

The nurse nodded towards the single rooms on their right. "Room 4, but if she's asleep please don't wake her– she's exhausted."

Albie led the way while Darcy promised a quick visit.

Shelley's small body under the hospital blankets gave her the appearance of a child half her age.

"Shelley," Albie smiled at her then nodded to her mother sitting in the chair next to the bed. "Angie." He and Darcy entered the room.

"How're you, Shelley?"

Shelley ignored Albie's question. Her face lit up with a smile. "Darcy, you came!"

Darcy sidestepped him and held Shelley's out-stretched hand. "Of course, I came."

Albie stared past them to Angie, walked around the bed and pulled up another chair "We're here to ask Shelley a few questions. Are you–"

"Whatever you need. I really don't know how to thank you. However, we can help." Angie dabbed her eyes with a shredded tissue. She leaned in and whispered, "I want that bastard out of my house. He touched my little–" Her sentence was swallowed by a gulp and more tears. Albie covered her hands with his, squeezed then nodded to Darcy.

"We found Sian, Shelley. Did you know?"

Shelley's nod was hardly visible, and she'd lowered her face looking at the thread from the blanket she twiddled between her tiny fingers.

"It's okay, Shelley," Darcy leaned forward and lifted her chin. "You've done nothing wrong. I wondered if you could tell me what happened."

"Okay," Shelley whispered.

"Why did you hide Sian?"

Shelley hesitated and glanced at Angie before answering. "I was frightened Billy would hurt Sian."

"What made you think Billy would hurt Sian?"

Albie could hear the tremor in her voice as she answered. "Because Sian told me he'd kept wanting her to sit on his lap. He'd told her she was his special princess."

She stopped and glanced at the three faces.

"Hmm...hmm...and?"

"He said he was going to spoil her tonight when mummy was asleep, and that's what he'd said to me before he—" Her bottom lip rolled, she sobbed.

Angie climbed onto the bed and wrapped Shelley in her arms. She crushed her body in her protective hold and buried her face in her little girl's hair.

Albie glanced back at the entwined bodies sitting up on the bed. "I'll text you when it's safe to go home."

9

———————

Albie smiled, a real dimpled smile, "Do you fancy seeing if Billy Stanton's home?"

A nod from Darcy was all he needed to turn left towards the estate. Although it was past eleven, the area was anything but quiet. The estate that never slept—Albie would have gone mad living here. He'd never be comfortable living his life to everyone else's beat. He watched Darcy slip her jacket over the ripped and bloodstained blouse. Superficial scratches and grazes, the paramedics said. She'd refused treatment, adamant she'd clean up at home.

"You'll do." He said, rounding the car and heading into the square. He killed the lights as he pulled into a visitor's space at the end of the road. One thing he knew for sure was that Billy Stanton had been running from the police most of his life. They needed the element of surprise. The front of the house was in darkness.

"Round the back." He led the way, half expecting a wasted journey.

Darcy edged behind him. "There's a light on in the kitchen. Shall we take a look?"

Before Albie moved, a door slammed. He stilled and listened to the clomp of footsteps, one footfall heavier than the other until they were within spitting distance.

"Billy Stanton, good to see you again."

DS Edwards stood directly in front of Billy as he stepped through the back garden gate. Billy bounced on his toes, his eyes wide, searching from side to side, looking for an escape. He rammed head first into Edward's stomach and knocked him backward. As Albie fell to the ground, Billy ran.

Darcy reacted instinctively. Darting forward, she took a flying jump and she crashed into the back of Billy's legs. He crashed to the ground, his arms flailing.

One more knee to the back of his legs kept him down as Albie got to his feet and came up to them.

"Great work, Nicholls." He held out his hand and helped her to her feet. He caught his breath and yanked Billy to his feet.

Billy yelled, "Piss off. Get your hands off me, filth."

Albie smiled as he jerked Billy's hands behind his back and tightened the cuffs. They led him back to the car. Albie read his rights and placed his hand on Billy's head as he lowered him into the seat.

"Billy Stanton, just the person we were hoping to see." Fawn walked towards them as they approached the duty sergeant. "It's been quite a day. Some of your friends stopped in for a chat. Oh, and just in case you're wondering, Shelley's doing fine and talking."

Billy ignored Fawn and continued to empty his pockets for the duty officer.

"Nothing to say, Billy? That's okay. Shelley can do the talking for you."

Billy cracked his fist on the counter and with a sneer turned to Fawn who stood behind Albie and Darcy.

"You've got nothing on me. She's a lying cow. Just ask her mother."

Spittle sprayed from his mouth. His face was contorted, his eyes like slits, the vein in his neck would burst if it stuck out any further.

Fawn grinned at Stanton's reaction, the first she'd seen since they'd marched him through the doors.

"See you later. Look forward to our chat." She backed towards the double doors. "Oh, and I wouldn't count on support from Angie Wilkins. Not now. You see, Sian. She didn't make it." She let the double doors spring back and watched through the glass as he strained against Albie's grip.

"You're talking shit. I didn't do nothing to Sian. You can't put that on me."

"Calm down unless you want me to add a charge of assaulting a police officer to the list." DS Peck, the duty sergeant, held one arm and nodded to another officer to hold the other until they reached the reinforced door.

Darcy slid down the wall, head in hands, and sobbed. Albie sat by her side and rubbed his hand in small circles over her shoulder and back.

"She's dead. We did all that, and Sian's dead."

"It's tragic, I know. He'll get his, and you'll get used to the job."

Darcy shook her head, wiped the back of her hand under her nose, and sniffed.

"No." Her body shook as she stood, and she supported herself with the wall. "I don't want to get used to this, hearing that a seven-year-old died because her sister tried to hide her from some pervert. It's not tragic... It's twisted."

Albie stood, holding out his hand to help steady her. "Go home, get some sleep. You'll feel differently in the morning. See you tomorrow."

She stopped and spluttered; wide tear trails etched in the dirt on her face. "You won't. Goodbye, DS Edwards."

For a moment, he thought about following her, talking some sense into her, but instead, he watched Peck escort Stanton to his cell. As the duty sergeant leant forward to unlock the cell door, Albie locked eyes with the girl's attacker. There was no doubt in his mind it was not the only label to fit Billy Stanton. He hoped Fawn found enough to put him away for a long time. Instead of lowering his gaze, Billy stared back. The corner of his mouth turned into a sneer, a challenge.

The first man who'd smiled at Albie with a challenge in his eye was his father—that night in the woods with the woman who resembled a bleeding angel.

10

A shudder ran down Albie's spine. He was on his knees in a squelch of mud and leaves. The silence terrified him as much as the woman's sobs and begging had earlier in the evening. He scanned the immediate area, but there was no sign of anything untoward, and for a moment, he questioned his own sanity. He knew he'd witnessed something horrific, but his father's involvement peppered his memories with disbelief. It caused Albie to disassociate from the pleas and screams that left him alone in this dreaded silence.

From behind the trees the men returned with muddied shovels over their shoulders. They passed close to the thicket, which was barely adequate coverage even for a small child of Albie's stature. His pulse quickened, and his body shook uncontrollably. A squeal left his lips, a sound like a wounded animal, and his need to run overwhelmed his common sense. He bolted.

"Stop." Freddie's shout was guttural and final. Albie froze.

"Jerry, take my son back to his mother."

Albie's shoulders relaxed, and he turned towards his father. He was surprised to see his father smile—forced perhaps, but still a smile.

"We'll just pretend you weren't here this evening, shall we? After all, I said no to seeing you tonight."

Albie mouthed 'sorry', but no sound came out.

"Oh, and happy birthday, son." His Father's words were an afterthought that stung Albie's heart. Freddie spoke in a low tone. "I think he's had his initiation. Let's go home."

Albie jogged away from the custody cells in the direction the duty sergeant pointed when he'd asked where Darcy had gone. He swung through the front doors and scanned the street until he spotted her walk into the newsagents opposite.

He sat on the top step outside the police station. It had been a traumatic day. Darcy had handled the investigation like a professional, and he so wanted the chance to praise her courage. If he saw her tomorrow, he'd make sure she knew she was valued. He sighed and rubbed his hands over his face; the day weighing on him.

A police car darted from a side street, lights flashing, and siren blaring. Albie watched as it zig-zagged in and out of the traffic and wondered what the poor blokes would find when they reached their destination. His hand knocked the packet of cigarettes in his jacket pocket, and he gave into temptation and lit up.

Jerry opened the boot and rearranged the content before ridding himself of the shovel and wiping his hands on an old cloth. He hummed a tune Albie thought familiar but couldn't quite recognise. He strode towards Albie and picked him off his

feet before opening the front passenger door and placing him on the seat. He climbed in the car and turned the engine over, switching on the heater, which made a melodic, soothing purring sound.

As the car drove away, Albie glanced at Jerry who tapped his fingers on the steering wheel to the beat of a song on the radio. Albie thought it was the Rolling Stones but couldn't be sure. Jerry didn't speak, although he occasionally glanced back at Albie and grinned, showing his teeth. A few metal caps glinted when the streetlights caught them.

Albie tried to temper his shaking body, cold from exposure and relenting to the overwhelming shock of the evening events. In one swift movement, Jerry angled his arm around the driver's seat and pulled a blanket from the back before whipping it over Albie's lap. Thanking the man under his breath, he snuggled under the blanket, which smelt musty, like they had stored it in a damp closet for years. But at least it wasn't too long before feeling tingled in his fingers again.

As they passed through the town, the streets became sleepier, and Albie found it difficult to keep his heavy eyelids open.

"Nearly home, young man." Jerry's voice pulled him from the brink of sleep. The wheels of the car bounced off the curb, just a few houses down from Albie's home. Jerry grasped his shoulder, and twisted Albie to face him.

"You've been on quite an adventure today, young Albie. It's best if you keep this to yourself. Don't want to go upsetting your mum now, do you?" Jerry winked and pointed to the street door. "Off you go. Don't forget our secret."

Before lifting the second house brick from the end, which bordered the flowers and hid the spare door key, Albie slowly turned full circle to ensure no one was watching him. It took a few attempts for Albie to grasp the key between his cold, numb fingers. Syncing the lock with his shaking hands was even more of a challenge. He replaced the key and tiptoed inside, squeezing through a narrow gap to stop the creak of the hinges. The light was on in the living room. The sounds of David Bowie reached his ear, as did the tearful tones of his mother's normally angelic singing voice, cracked by her sobs. He peeked inside and watched her sway back and forth–her back to him and a glass of wine in her hand. David Bowie sang about 'Sorrow' while his mother epitomised the very emotion.

Albie slid past and took the stairs with a nimble tread, unclear of exactly what he'd witnessed on the evening of his seventh birthday. Albie threw himself onto his bed. His shoulders shuddered and he sobbed uncontrollably. He was home. He was safe.

Albie inhaled a final drag of his cigarette then threw it to the curb. He shook his head. Staring after Darcy as she walked away in the distance, he wondered if he would ever see her again. Albie pulled the packet of cigarettes from his pocket and crumpled it in his fist destroying the whole pack. Breathing deeply, he wiped his misty eyes and swallowed a lump in his throat. Albie sighed, thinking of the boy he once was. He knew deep down that some memories were best left buried. As he turned to go back into the station, he threw the crumpled packet of cigarettes into the nearest rubbish bin.

ACKNOWLEDGMENTS

Thank you to the wonderful people who have provided invaluable input to *Buried Memories* and who kept me sane through the creative process. My husband, Roy, and my children, Dan, Lee, Samantha, Ben, Steven and Luke who listened to me ramble on incoherently as I thought through the plot and story arcs.

To Tricia Humphries for her keen eye and talent for teaching me strategies to stop me head hopping! First readers, Colin Apps and Yvonne for keeping my eye on the finishing line.

Special thanks to Rod Gilley, you questioned everything and helped me to form my ideas into something cohesive for my readers.

Thanks to Annemarie, Donna and Dragonflygrl4ever for your feedback on REAM you are the best!

To my readers, I send a massive thank you for taking time out of your busy life to read *Buried Memories*.

If you enjoyed the story, please consider writing a review at your favourite retailers and remember to tell your friends about the book.

You can find the link to stores here: https://books2read.com/u/b6YZX6

ABOUT THE AUTHOR

Kimberley Shead writes stories that explore humanity, morality, and the human psyche. She writes dark crime and psychological thrillers set in England. Every story she shares evokes emotion and includes characters who will stay with you long after you close the final page.

Kimberley lives in London, England with her husband and German Shepherd dog, Rex.

Find out more about Kimberley here: www.kimberleyshead.com

THE VOYEUR
CHAPTER 1

DS Albie Edwards surveyed the scene from the edge of the woods. Chaos. At least, that's how an outsider would see it. But Albie knew better.

He stooped, knelt on his right knee in the gravel, and winced as he rubbed his left ankle. It was only a tweak, but even so, it pained him. Serves me right, he thought. After all, what had he expected to gain from jumping out of a moving vehicle?

Tanya would scold him when she caught up, and she'd be right. He should have been patient and waited while she found a parking space.

Albie stood and elbowed a pathway through the gathering crowd. He'd come to associate those who gathered at crime scenes as hyenas—excited and alert for information like meagre pickings after an attack. He shielded his eyes from the sun and scanned the trees. Sure enough, kids perched on the branches. They hustled for position and the best vantage point, each desperate for a glimpse of a corpse.

"Get those kids down from the trees," Albie ordered a fresh-faced police officer standing behind the crime scene tape, that she guarded like a German Shepherd does its master.

"Straight away, Sarge." The officer stood to attention as she eyed his ID card and spoke to his back as he trudged towards the area shaded by a canopy of branches. He picked his way through a tangle of brambles and tall swaying nettles, then stopped on the outskirts of the undergrowth and observed his colleagues searching the area in sombre silence.

A moment later, he heard the boys from the trees, grumbling and shouting abuse to the officer who hurried them away.

A rustle in the bushes to his right caught his attention. His dishevelled colleague moved closer.

"Thanks for waiting." She said, as she swiped prickles and stingers from her chestnut curls.

"Sort yourself out, Watts. I thought you were in tiptop condition." Albie covered his smile with his hand and strode towards the bright lights. "Follow me."

PC Tanya Watts bent forward and waited for her short, shallow breaths to slow.

"Yes, that's right. I've been mucking about," she mumbled. "It's funny that, because I feel like I've run 100 metres so as not to be left behind." She sucked in a deep breath, forced her body upright, and followed at a distance.

Albie stifled a grin at her sarcasm. It had taken time to build trust in their working relationship. They were only five substantial cases into their partnership, but for some reason it worked.

The white tent stood alive with shadows.

If he played the association game, tents for Albie would equate to childhood fun; camping holidays by the sea, adventures in the back garden, secret meeting places, and long hot summers.

How easily childhood memories were shattered.

He studied the area and knew once he entered that tent, another nail would be hammered into the heart of the boy he once was, the boy who'd suffered from a slow cruel death which began at the site of his first murder scene.

Now a white tent meant death.

"Ah, DS Edwards and the lovely Ms Watts." A gravel-edged voice came from the far corner of the tent, followed by an exaggerated cough. Both officers tried to identify the hunched figure as he straightened and stretched. A bright lamp contorted his appearance. "I wish I could say it's a pleasure to have your company, but I think, under these circumstances, it would be a false sentiment."

"Leo." Albie outstretched his hand in greeting and waited for the forensic pathologist to place fibres into an evidence bag before he responded.

"So, how are you both?" Leo asked, his focus on Tanya.

Tanya nodded and averted her eyes. Albie smiled as she fumbled in her jacket pocket and pulled out a notebook and pen. He knew it was routine for her to record every detail. At a later date, she'd find those buried clues, the game winners.

"All good," Albie answered for Tanya and himself. "So, what can you tell us?"

Leo removed his gloves, placed a hand on Tanya's shoulder, and leaned behind her to find a replacement pair. She angled away from his touch but continued to scribble in her notebook while they focused on the victim.

From a distance, the large object nestled in a bed of nettles and weeds was hidden, camouflaged with leaves in a shamble of autumnal shades. Known as a local dumping ground, it featured a place for broken, worn, and unwanted objects to languish into a slow death.

And a discarded carpet was not an unusual sight. The fringe of the carpet splayed across the soil and entwined with dank clumps of dark brown hair while, at the opposite end of the bundle, limp, pale toes with party-painted nails were barely visible. The carpet was frayed, with bald patches and splashes of dirt-ridden flowers. Whatever the carpet's original use, the killer had fastened the distasteful packaging to secure the corpse, and fastened it secured with a one-inch thick rope in an olive hue.

"Cut the rope." Albie's attempt to control the tremor in his voice and the shaking in his forearm was a reaction to the anxiety and anticipation that battled inside him for the right to the highest status in his body.

Leo slipped a flick knife with a mother-of-pearl style shell handle and a razor-sharp edge between the carpet and the rope. Albie watched Leo's precise sawing motion, small smooth movements. Breathing heavily, Albie knelt by the victim's pale feet, too clean to have touched the moist soil.

"Have you got another knife in your bag of tricks?" Albie asked as he searched a nearby bag.

Leo stopped, gave Albie his knife, and grabbed his bag from Albie's grasp. Within seconds, he'd found a smaller knife in a hidden zip pocket and continued the slow process of freeing the body while Albie focused on slicing through another part of the rope.

He shook his head and grinned. "Some things never change, do they, mate? As impatient as ever. Just take it easy. Remember, she's dead. There's nothing we can do to help her except make sure we keep all the evidence intact." Leo continued sawing his piece of rope when Albie slowed down.

The process was monotonous and time-consuming, and Albie could only watch as Leo cut the final length of rope.

Finished with the notebook and pen, Tanya put them away as Leo drew the knife through the final tether, and the rope broke free.

All three took up positions beside the body. Each took a deep breath, fingered the edge of the carpet, and moved backwards on their haunches. They peeled it back, careful not to disturb the contents. The taste of rotten flesh hit the back of their throats as they gulped shallow breaths. Albie's eyes watered against the violent intrusion of death he knew would cling to his body for days. The trio moved in silence to the opposite side of the bundle to repeat the process.

Albie shoved his hands in his pockets and tried to ignore his quickening pulse. He shuffled from foot to foot and made a conscious effort not to bite the raw hangnail on his thumb. He reminded himself they'd just unwrapped a corpse.

"Okay, she's ready for you," Leo said unravelliing the carpet that had proved harder to remove.

Tanya stepped behind Albie, notebook and pen poised once again. It took time to build trust in a working relationship. As far as Albie was concerned, he had complete trust in Tanya Watts. They were only five substantial cases into their partnership, but for some reason it worked.

At first glance, the bulk of the victim's body was disguised, hidden under a throw of orange, red, and brown mulched leaves, mildew damp—crude clothing nature offered as a cover for her nakedness. Under the leaves, her skin bore a translucent sheen mottled with dark patches and open wounds where parasites had laid eggs and feasted on the flesh of their host.

Leo peeled pulp from her face and neck with patient

precision and distributed samples into small plastic sealed evidence bags.

Albie edged forwards and knelt on the sheet beside the body. Entwined around her neck was soiled cloth. A thin piece of metal poked upwards. The end dug into her chin.

"Is that a bra?" Albie asked.

Tanya stepped nearer, and Leo picked at the lace edge with his tweezers. "Move that light, will you?"

Albie leaned on one knee and groaned at the clicks as he eased himself to his feet. He stood behind the light and struggled with the frame. Then he manoeuvred it until the lamp lit the woman's torso. He lowered his head, unsure whether he did so out of respect or repulsion. He glanced at Tanya as she stared at the damage left by this woman's abuser. He filled his lungs with tainted air and followed her gaze.

"Do you notice the marks carved into her chest? These were made postmortem ." Leo swept his gloved fingers between the slashes. "She needs cleaning up to know if they're of any significance."

"I've seen enough. Need fresh air." Tanya said.

Albie noted the puce tone to her skin and watched in silence as she navigated the tent flap and slipped out on his nod.

"She all right?" Leo didn't look up, but concern was clear in his voice.

"Sure. We've been here a while. Probably seen too much. Notice her arm?" Leo turned his attention to the bruised tracks on the fragile skin of the victim's inner arm.

"It's not surprising. Vulnerable addict, easy prey." Albie said, staring at the corpse.

"Look, this is going to take time." Leo turned to Albie.

"Why don't you check on PC Watts? I'll be in touch when I have more to tell you," Leo said.

Albie stared at the victim's face–a mask. He'd never know the true terror of her ordeal, and not for the first time, Albie wished the dead could talk.

www.ingramcontent.com/pod-product-compliance
Lightning Source LLC
Chambersburg PA
CBHW021136130726
47988CB00003B/1325